Wait for the silence of the night and listen
for the nightingale.

For Maroun from Beni

HANS CHRISTIAN ANDERSEN
THE NIGHTINGALE
ILLUSTRATED BY BENI MONTRESOR

Adapted by Alan Benjamin

CROWN PUBLISHERS, INC.   NEW YORK

Illustrations copyright © 1985 by Beni Montressor. All rights reserved. Published by Crown Publishers, Inc., One Park Avenue, New York, New York 10016 and simultaneously in Canada by General Publishing Company Limited. Manufactured in Japan. CROWN is a trademark of Crown Publishers, Inc. Library of Congress Cataloging in Publication Data. Benjamin, Alan. Hans Christian Andersen's the nightingale. Adaptation of: Nattergalen. Summary: Despite being neglected by the emperor for a jewel-studded bird, the little nightingale revives the dying ruler with its beautiful song.   [1. Fairy tales]   I. Andersen, H. C. (Hans Christian), 1805-1875. Nattergalen.   II. Montresor, Beni, ill.   III. Title. PZ8.B4258   1984   [E]   83-23956   ISBN 0-517-55211-6   First Edition   10 9 8 7 6 5 4 3 2 1

T he story I am about to tell you happened long, long ago. It's for that very reason I want you to hear it now—so it won't be forgotten.

The Emperor of China lived in a palace more splendid than any other in the world. It was fashioned of gleaming porcelain, so fine and so fragile that light could pass through its gilded walls. The palace gardens were filled with the rarest of flowers, some of which were hung with tiny silver bells that trembled and tinkled in the breeze, so that no one could pass by without noticing them. The gardens stretched so far in every direction that not even the chief gardener knew where they ended.

If you wandered long enough, or far enough, you would find yourself in a forest whose towering trees were mirrored in a hundred glittering lakes. Among these trees lived a nightingale. Her song was so sweet that even the poor fisherman, who had much else to think about, would stop to listen while drawing in his nets at night.

Travelers from all over the world came to marvel at the Emperor's city, his palace, and his gardens. But when they heard the song of the nightingale, they all agreed that this was indeed the greatest marvel of them all. When they returned home, they told all who would listen about the wonders they had seen, and the cleverest of them wrote poems about their travels.

These poems went all over the world, and one of them finally reached the Emperor. He smiled with pleasure at the glowing descriptions of his royal domain. "But of all the Emperor's treasures," he read, "none is finer than the nightingale."

"The nightingale!" he exclaimed. "What nightingale? I know nothing of it, and yet it lives in my very own garden!" And with that, he summoned his prime minister.

"I have read that there is a wonderful bird living in our gardens—a nightingale," he began. "Why do I know nothing of it?"

"I know nothing of it myself Your Highness," replied the prime minister. "It has never been presented at court."

"Be that as it may," said the Emperor. "I command that it be presented to me this evening so that I, too, may hear its song."

"I will find the bird at once, Your Majesty," said the prime minister. Then upstairs and downstairs he ran, and in and out of all the rooms and corridors of the palace. He questioned everyone he met, but no one had ever heard of the nightingale. So back he hurried to the Emperor, saying that it must be nothing but a myth, invented by the writer of the poem. "Your Majesty should not believe everything he reads," counseled the prime minister.

"Nonsense!" replied the Emperor. "The poem was sent to me by the almighty Emperor of Japan himself, so it must be true. Now listen, and listen well....I will hear the nightingale sing tonight, or everyone in the palace will be punished."

"As you command," said the prime minister, and off he ran again. After questioning everyone he met for a second time, he still had no knowledge of where the bird might be found. Exhausted, he went to the palace kitchen for a cup of tea. A poor kitchen maid, scrubbing the royal pots and pans, overheard him discussing his problem with the chief cook. "I know the nightingale well," she said. "Every evening I am allowed to take some table scraps to my sick old mother who lives in the forest. On my way back to the palace, I stop to rest for awhile, and it's then that I hear her beautiful song."

"My child," said the prime minister, "if you will take us to the nightingale, I will give you permission to watch our beloved Emperor dine. He has commanded that the bird be brought to him tonight."

So off they went—the kitchen maid, the prime minister, and half the court. When they had gone a little way into the forest, a cow began to bellow.

"Listen!" said a gentleman-in-waiting. "That must be it. What incredible power for such a little creature."

"No," said the kitchen maid, "that's only a cow. We still have a long way to go." Then some frogs began to croak in the marsh.

"How delicate," sighed a lady of the court, "like the sound of little bells."

"Those are only frogs," said the kitchen maid, "but we are almost there."

Just then, the nightingale began to sing.

"There she is," said the kitchen maid, and she pointed to a little gray bird, high up in the branches.

"Amazing!" said the prime minister. "I didn't think she would be so ordinary looking." Then, raising his voice so the bird could hear him, he declared, "My dear little nightingale, I have the honor to invite you to the palace this evening. His Imperial Majesty, the Emperor of China, wishes to hear your enchanting voice."

"My singing really sounds better in the open air," said the nightingale. "But I will be happy to accompany you if that is the Emperor's wish."

At the palace, everything had been scrubbed and polished until the porcelain walls and floors gleamed in the light of a thousand golden lamps. Flowers, hung with tiny bells, had been arranged in all the rooms and corridors; and there was such a breeze from all the hurrying and scurrying that the bells were set a-tinkling. In the middle of the throne room, the nightingale had been set on a golden perch. The entire court was there, dressed in their finest, and even the little kitchen maid had been allowed to watch from behind a door. Everyone's eyes were on the little gray bird as the Emperor motioned for her to begin.

The nightingale sang so enchantingly that tears came to the Emperor's eyes and rolled down his imperial cheeks. He was so pleased that he offered the nightingale his golden slipper to wear around her neck. But the nightingale declined, saying, "Thank you, but I have been rewarded enough. I can think of no richer prize than an emperor's tears."

Everyone agreed that the nightingale had been a great sensation. She was to remain at court and to have her own cage. She was granted permission to go out walking twice a day and once at night. On these walks, she was accompanied by twelve footmen who each held on to a silken ribbon tied 'round her leg. Of course there was little pleasure for the nightingale in these outings.

The whole city talked of nothing but this remarkable bird. When two people met, one of them would merely utter "night" and the other "gale." Then they would both sigh, completely understanding each other. At least eleven shopkeepers' children were named for the delightful creature, but not even one could sing a note.

One day a package arrived for the Emperor. On the outside was written the word "Nightingale." The Emperor imagined it was another book about his celebrated bird, but he was wrong. Inside the box lay a remarkable toy—a mechanical nightingale encrusted with diamonds, rubies and sapphires. One had only to wind it up, and it would flap its glittering wings and tail and sing one of the songs the real nightingale sang.

Everyone was very taken with the mechanical bird, and the one who had brought it was immediately given the title of Chief-Imperial-Nightingale Carrier.

"Now they must sing together," said the prime minister. "What a glorious duet that will be."

So the two birds sang together, but it was not a success. The real bird sang in her own way, changing the melody according to her fancy, but the song of the other was completely mechanical. "There's nothing wrong with that," said the royal music master. "It keeps perfect time, and is correct in every way."

After that, the Emperor had the mechanical bird sing alone. It was soon as popular as the living one and was, of course, much prettier, glittering as it did like a cluster of brooches and bracelets.

Over and over again it sang its one and only song, three and thirty times without tiring. Then the Emperor thought it was time for the real nightingale to sing again. But where was she? No one had noticed when she flew out the open window and back to her own green forest. The Emperor and all his courtiers agreed that she was a most ungrateful bird.

"Still," they said, "we have the best of the two," and with that, they wound up the mechanical bird again. And for the thirty-fourth time they heard the same song. The music master heaped praise on the jeweled bird, declaring it better than the living one, not only for its outward appearance, but for the wonderful clockwork within.

Everyone agreed, and the music master was given permission to show the bird to the public on the following Sunday. When they heard it sing, they oohed and aahed and drank themselves merry on tea. But the fisherman, who had heard the real nightingale sing, said, "It's a pretty song indeed, but something just seems to be missing."

The real nightingale was banished from the kingdom forever, and the mechanical bird was given a place on a silken cushion, close to the Emperor's bed.

Things went on this way for an entire year, until the Emperor, his court, and all the people of the city knew every chirp and gurgle of the mechanical bird by heart. Then one evening, as the Emperor lay in bed listening to his jeweled bird, there was a sudden whizzing and whirring from inside the creature, and the singing stopped.

The Emperor leaped from his bed and sent for his physicians, but they could do nothing. Then the royal watchmaker was summoned. After a great deal of poking and prodding, he announced that the mechanical bird would never sing again.

Five years passed, and then a great sadness fell over the land. The Emperor was ill, and it was said he would not live much longer. All the floors in the palace had been covered with thick carpets, so that no one's footsteps would disturb the dying Emperor. A new emperor had been chosen, and many at court, believing the old Emperor to be dead already, were paying their respects to the new one.

But the Emperor was not dead yet. Pale and still he lay and could barely breathe. He felt as if something were weighing on his chest. He opened his eyes and, indeed, Death was sitting there, wearing the Emperor's golden crown. In one hand he held the Emperor's sword, and in the other, the imperial banner. From the folds of the great velvet curtains that surrounded the bed peered many faces—some kind, some frighteningly ugly. These were the Emperor's good and evil deeds.

"Do you remember this?" and "Do you remember that?" they whispered, reminding him of past deeds that made him tremble with fear.

"Enough!" he shouted. "Music! Sound the great gong that I may not hear what they're saying!" But still they went on, as Death sat nodding his head. "Music!" cried the Emperor again. "My wonderful little bird, sing, sing! I have showered you with precious gifts. Now sing, I tell you, sing!"

But the broken bird was silent, and Death continued to stare at the Emperor with dark hollow eyes. Then, suddenly, came a burst of the most beautiful singing. It was the living nightingale, perched on a tree outside the window. She had heard of the Emperor's suffering, and had come to comfort him. As she sang, the faces in the draperies grew fainter and fainter, while the face of the Emperor flushed with new color and vigor. Death himself listened to her song and said, "Go on little nightingale, go on!"

"I will," answered the nightingale, "if you will give me the Emperor's sword…his banner…his crown."

And Death gave up each treasure for a song. The nightingale sang of the peaceful graveyard where white roses bloom, where elder blossoms perfume the air, and where the grass is ever freshened by the tears of those left behind. Death began to long for his own garden and, like a cold gray mist, drifted out the window.

"Thank you, my beloved little bird," said the Emperor. "Though I banished you from my kingdom, you have lifted Death from my heart. How can I ever repay you?"

"You have done so already," said the nightingale. "The first time I sang for you, I brought tears to your eyes. Those are the jewels that gladden a singer's heart. But sleep now and regain your strength. I will sing to you."

Then the nightingale sang again, and the Emperor fell into a deep, sweet sleep. When he awoke, with the sun streaming in through the window, he felt completely recovered. None of his servants had yet come back, because they believed the Emperor to be dead, but the nightingale continued to sing outside his window.

"You must never leave me again," said the Emperor, "but you shall sing only when you wish."

"I cannot make my home in your palace," said the nightingale, "but I will come from time to time to sing outside your window. I will sing to cheer you, and to make you thoughtful as well. I will sing of those who are happy, and of those who suffer. I will sing of the good and of the evil that both surround you. I must fly far and wide, to the poor fisherman, and to the homes of peasants far from you and your court. Remember that I love your heart better than your crown. Yes, I will come and sing to you, but you must promise me one thing."

"Anything you ask," said the Emperor, standing now in his imperial robes and holding his golden sword against his heart.

"I ask only that you tell no one that you have a little bird who tells you everything." And with that, the nightingale flew away.

Moments later, the servants came in to prepare their dead Emperor for burial, and there he stood and bid them all "Good morning!"